For Heather —D. U.

For Kai and Ries —M. H.

Library of Congress Cataloging-in-Publication Data available.

ISBN 978-1-4521-7130-2

Manufactured in China.

Design by Jay Marvel.
Typeset in Sangli.
The illustrations in this book were rendered in brush and ink, pastel, marker, and graphite and colored digitally.

10 9 8 7 6 5 4 3 2 1

Chronicle books and gifts are available at special quantity discounts to corporations, professional associations, literacy programs, and other organizations. For details and discount information, please contact our premiums department at corporatesales@chroniclebooks.com or at 1-800-759-0190.

Chronicle Books LLC
680 Second Street
San Francisco, California 94107

Chronicle Books—we see things differently.
Become part of our community at www.chroniclekids.com.

JO BRIGHT
AND THE SEVEN BOTS

By Deborah Underwood
Illustrated by Meg Hunt

chronicle books · san francisco

Once upon a planetoid,
surrounded by her friends,
a girl, Jo Bright, loved building bots
from scraps and odds and ends.

The queen refused to let Jo use
her tools and bot supplies,

so Jo built bots from things she found
and learned to improvise.

The jealous, robot-building queen
watched Jo with irritation.
"Oh well—her bots will never match
my brilliant new creation."

"My mirror-bot must tell the truth.
Let's put it to the test!
Of all the planet's bot-builders,
do tell us: Who's the best?"

The mirror-bot replied, "My queen,
your bots are great, 'tis true,
but Jo Bright has become
a better bot-builder than you."

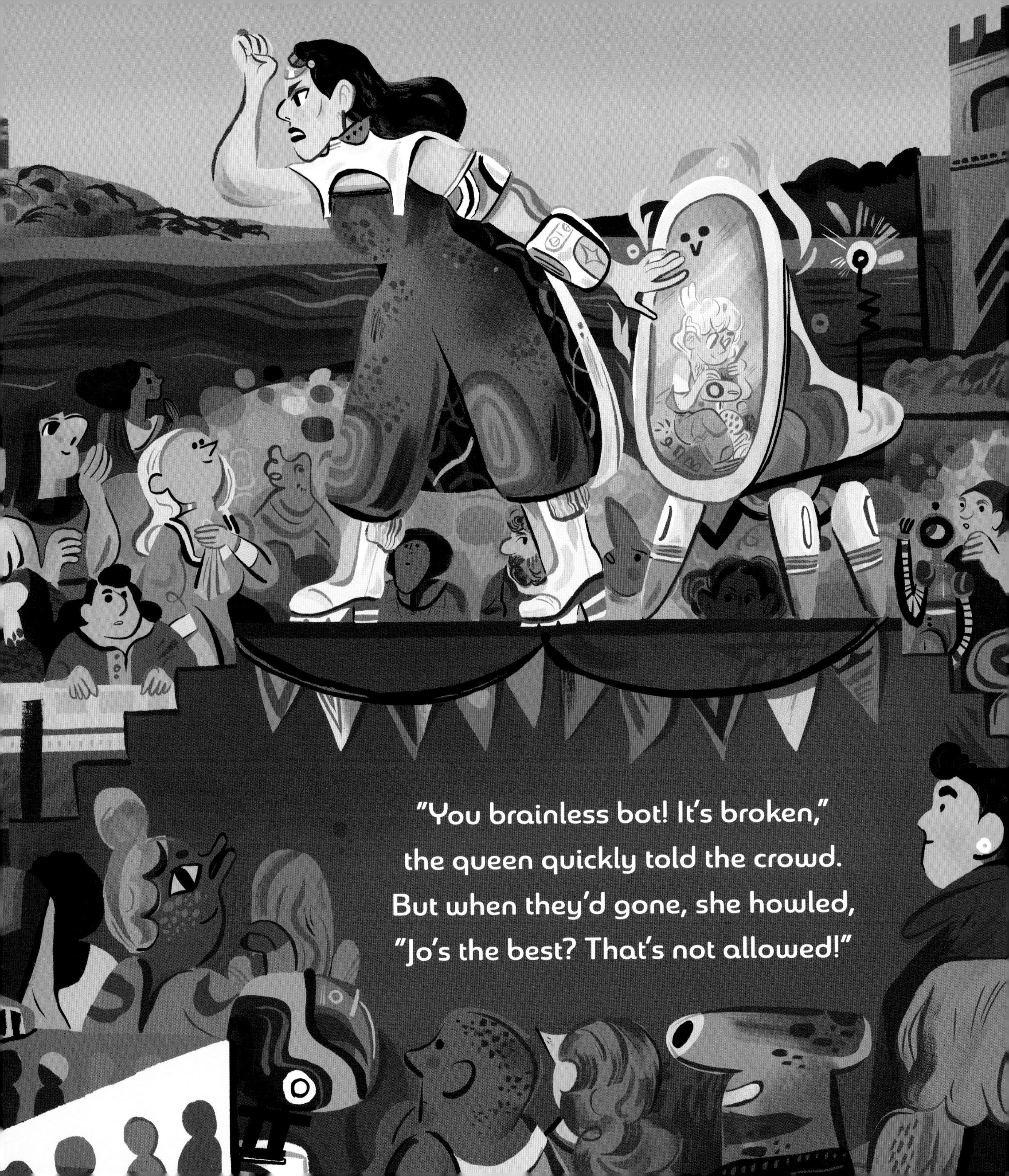

"You brainless bot! It's broken,"
the queen quickly told the crowd.
But when they'd gone, she howled,
"Jo's the best? That's not allowed!"

She scooped Jo up. "I'll drop you near the dreadful dragon's lair!"

Jo landed with a thump.
"I need a place to hide—ah! There!"

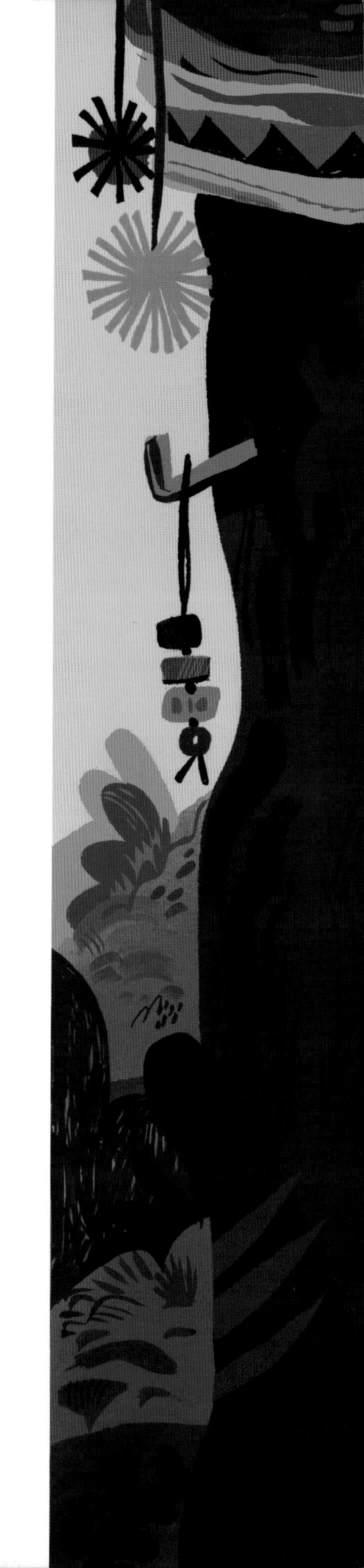

As Jo approached the mansion
she heard noises up above.
A shaky dragon voice called out,
"A child! Come in, my love!"

"But aren't you going to eat me?"

"Well, of course not. Goodness me!
I'm mostly vegetarian.
I'm Sparky. Come have tea!"

"The humans that I've met before
were all so full of fear.
Your queen kept trying to slay me,
so I've lived my life out here.

"But I've been lonely all these years,"
sobbed Sparky with a yelp.

"Well, you've got seven power packs.
Let's make some bots—come help!"

Soon Sparky's empty house was full
of bots to chat and sit with,
to garden and play dragon chess,
to walk and cook and knit with.

"Am I the best bot-builder NOW?"
The mirror-bot said, "No.
The best bot-builder's living with
a dragon—yes, it's Jo."

The raging ruler screamed and
smashed the mirror on its head.
"I'll make an evil apple-bot
and zap her till she's dead!"

The zapping apple, shiny red,
flew to the dragon's gate.

"Oh no!" cried Jo. "Don't touch it!"
But alas, she was too late.

The smallest dragon-bot was zapped!
He toppled to the ground.
His friends wept silver robot tears
and gathered close around.

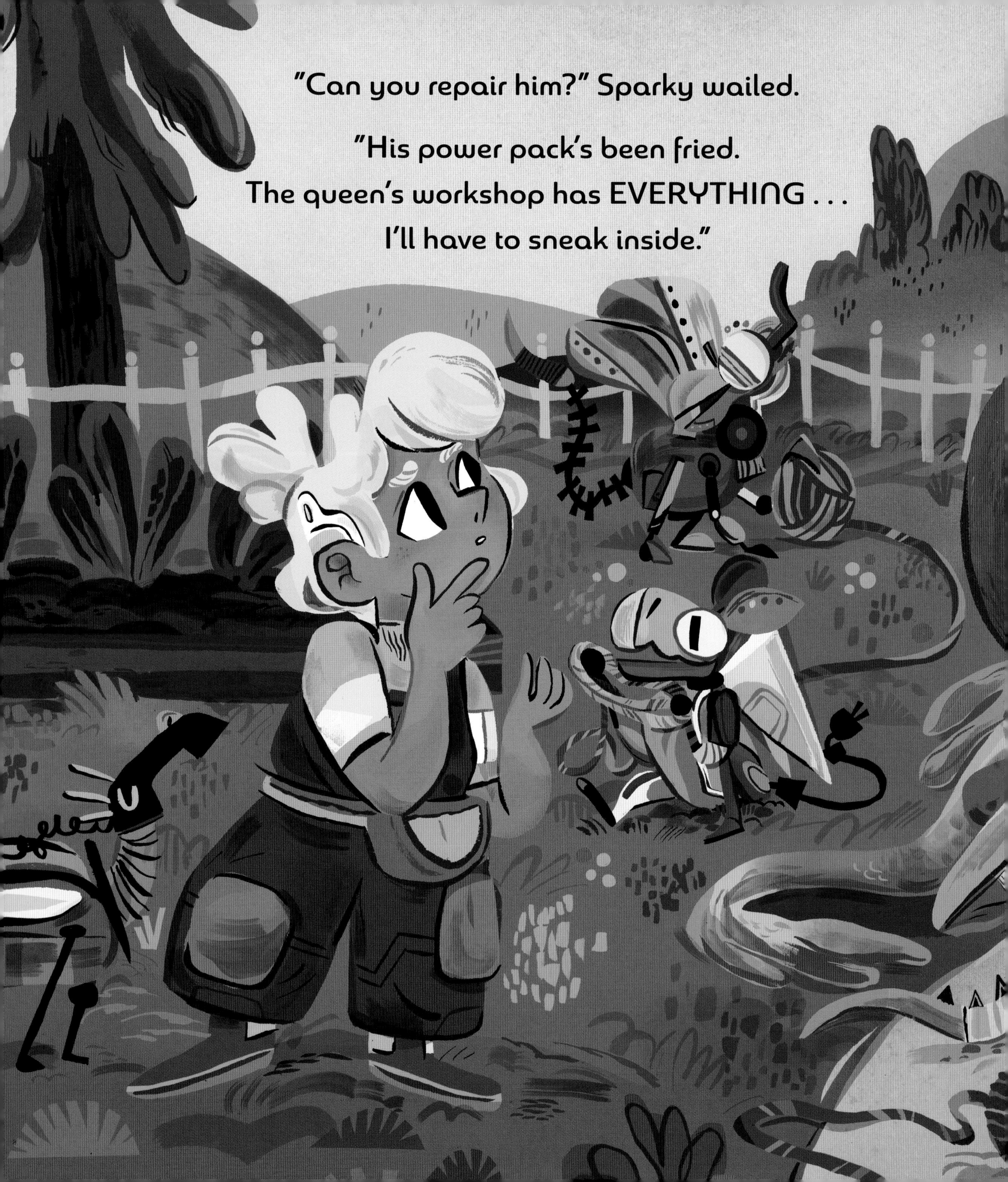

"Can you repair him?" Sparky wailed.

"His power pack's been fried.
The queen's workshop has EVERYTHING . . .
I'll have to sneak inside."

"We're coming with you," Sparky said.
The bots agreed, "You bet!"
Jo said, "There might be trouble,
so can you please knit a net?"

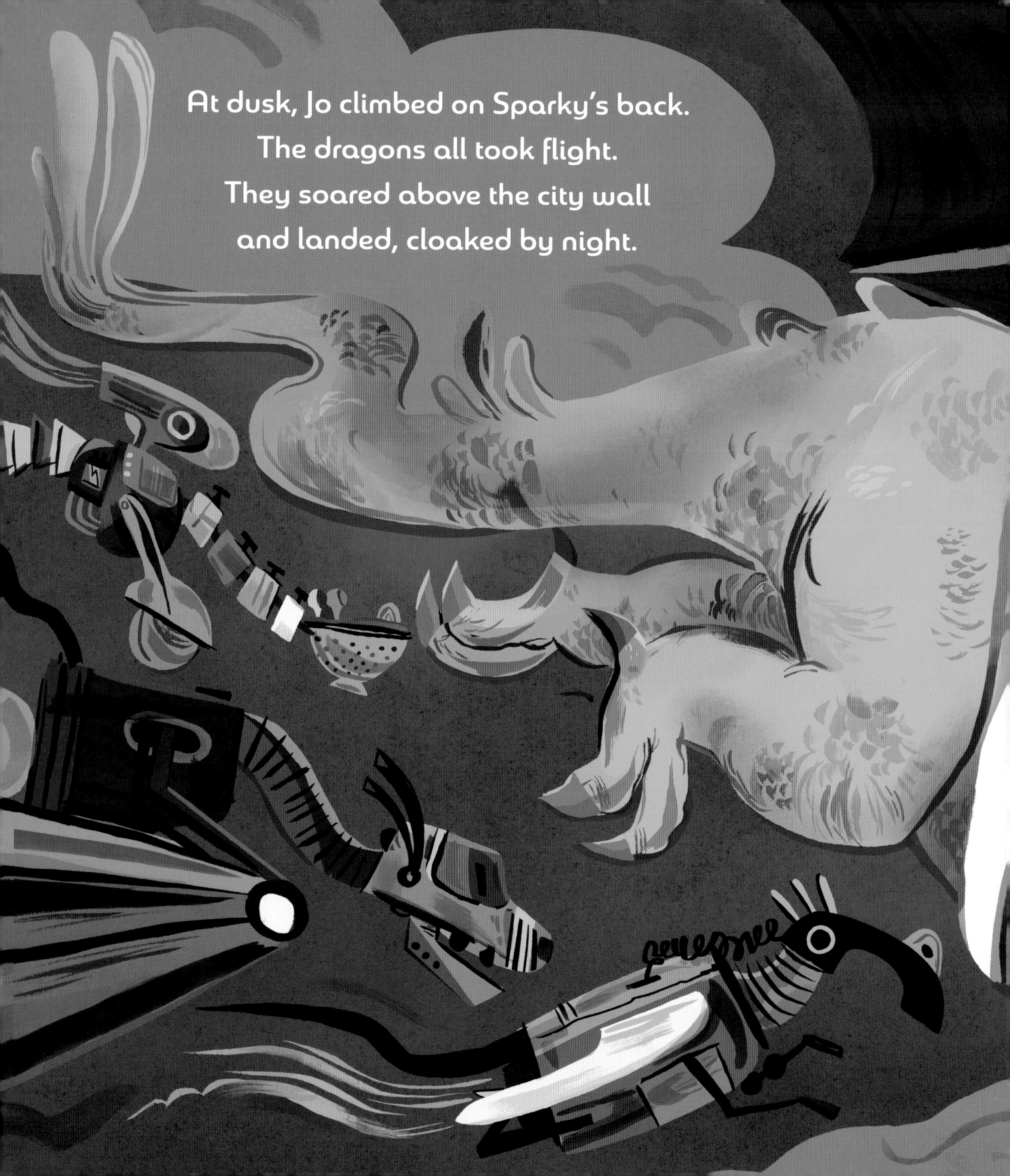

At dusk, Jo climbed on Sparky's back.
The dragons all took flight.
They soared above the city wall
and landed, cloaked by night.

Jo searched the workshop for a pack.
"However will I find it?"
She peered around a chest
and saw the mirror, smashed, behind it.

"Poor mirror-bot! I'll help you.
Then I'll bet you can help *me*!"
She fixed it fast and turned it on.
The mirror gasped, "QUEEN! FLEE!"

Alas, it was too late to hide.
The queen burst in. "You pest!
At last I can destroy you,
and I'll finally be the best!"

"Bots! NOW!" Jo called. The dragon-bots
swooped in and swarmed the shop.
They dropped the net and caught the queen,
who screamed, "You monsters! Stop!"

Then Sparky grabbed the captured queen
and soared into the air.

"Please fly her to the moon—
she'll be the best bot-builder there!"

"But who should rule our planet now?"

"The mirror-bot will know!"

"Your ruler must be smart and kind.
All hail your new queen: Jo!"

The new queen's coronation feast
had many an honored guest.

Jo ruled in peace and built with friends—

that truly *was* the best.